# BONES
## and the CLOWN MIX-UP Mystery

A Viking Easy-to-Read

BY DAVID A. ADLER

ILLUSTRATED BY BARBARA JOHANSEN NEWMAN

VIKING

For Jacob and Yoni, two great detectives! —D.A.

For my son, Mike. I'm very proud of you. —B.J.N.

VIKING
Published by Penguin Group
Penguin Young Readers Group, 345 Hudson Street, New York, New York 10014, U.S.A.
Penguin Group (Canada), 90 Eglinton Avenue East, Suite 700, Toronto, Ontario, Canada M4P 2Y3
(a division of Pearson Penguin Canada Inc.)
Penguin Books Ltd, 80 Strand, London WC2R 0RL, England
Penguin Ireland, 25 St Stephen's Green, Dublin 2, Ireland (a division of Penguin Books Ltd)
Penguin Group (Australia), 250 Camberwell Road, Camberwell, Victoria 3124, Australia
(a division of Pearson Australia Group Pty Ltd)
Penguin Books India Pvt Ltd, 11 Community Centre,
Panchsheel Park, New Delhi – 110 017, India
Penguin Group (NZ), 67 Apollo Drive, Rosedale, North Shore 0632,
New Zealand (a division of Pearson New Zealand Ltd)
Penguin Books (South Africa) (Pty) Ltd, 24 Sturdee Avenue, Rosebank,
Johannesburg 2196, South Africa

Penguin Books Ltd, Registered Offices: 80 Strand, London WC2R 0RL, England

First published in 2010 by Viking, a division of Penguin Young Readers Group

1  3  5  7  9  10  8  6  4  2

Text copyright © David A. Adler, 2010
Illustrations copyright © Barbara Johansen Newman, 2010

LIBRARY OF CONGRESS CATALOGING-IN-PUBLICATION DATA
Adler, David A.
Bones and the clown mix-up mystery / by David A. Adler ;
illustrated by Barbara Johansen Newman.
p. cm.— (Bones ; #8)
Summary: Detective Jeffrey Bones helps a clown who performed at his friend's birthday party
to find some lost clothing.
ISBN 978-0-670-06344-4 (hardcover)
[1. Mystery and detective stories. 2. Clowns—Fiction. 3. Lost and found possessions—Fiction.
4. Birthdays—Fiction.] I. Newman, Barbara Johansen, ill. II. Title.
PZ7.A2615Bod 2010
[E]—dc22
2009019204

Set in Bookman Light     Manufactured in China

# -CONTENTS-

# 1. Even Great Detectives Forget

There were dark clouds in the sky,

so I knew it was going to rain.

I put on my waterproof parka.

Dad put on his raincoat.

He was taking me to

Not-Me Amy's birthday party.

When you meet her, you'll know why

I call her "Not Me" Amy.

Dad reached into his pocket.

"Hey," he said. "Where are my keys?"

"I know it's going to rain," I said,

"and I know where to find your keys."

There were no dark clouds this morning,

so Dad wore his not-raining coat.

I found Dad's keys

in the pocket of his not-raining coat.

My name is Jeffrey Bones.

I find things. I solve mysteries.

"You find things," Dad said.

"You also forget things."

He was right. I had forgotten my detective bag.

"Didn't you forget something else?"

I looked in the bag.

My detective things were all there.

Dad said, "You forgot Amy's birthday gift."

He was right again. Even great detectives forget.

I got the gift.

We were ready to go to Not-Me Amy's party.

## 2. Toot! Toot! Toot!

Not-Me Amy's mother opened the door.

"Hello," I said. I put my parka

on a chair. Amy's mother said,

"Coats don't belong on chairs."

She put my parka in the closet.

I went to the den.

I gave Not-Me Amy the gift.

Jane said, "I brought a gift, too."

"Not me," Not-Me Amy said.

Of course she didn't bring a gift.

*It's her birthday!*

I sat between Jane and Tom.

I put my detective bag under my chair.

Amy's dad gave pizza to Not-Me Amy.

"Who else wants pizza?" he asked.

"I do! I do! I do!" we all said.

"Not me!" Not-Me Amy said.

"I already have pizza."

She always says, "Not me."

That's why I call her Not-Me Amy.

Amy's mom brought in a cake.

We all sang "Happy Birthday."

Not-Me Amy blew out the candles.

Amy's mom gave me a piece of cake.

I picked it up and took a big bite.

"Use your fork," Amy's mom told me.

"First," I said, "I have to clean my hands."

I licked off the icing. YUMMY!

"Use your napkin," Amy's mom said.

I did. I made a paper airplane.

Then Not-Me Amy opened her gifts.

I gave her a detective glass.

"It's good for finding things," I said.

*Toot! Toot! Toot!*

"Hey, what's that noise?" Tom asked.

*Toot! Toot! Toot!*

"Look," Jane said.

"It's a clown."

The clown had lots of

curly green-and-purple hair.

She reached behind Not-Me Amy's ear.

She pulled out a coin.

The clown held up the coin.

It was a dime.

"Yay!" we shouted.

The clown closed her hand and opened it.

The dime was gone.

"Yay!" we shouted.

The clown reached behind my ear.

She pulled out the dime and gave it to Amy.

I checked both my ears.

I hoped to find some coins.

I could use them to buy detective things.

My ears were empty.

"Hey," the clown asked.

"Who wants a rabbit?"

She blew up a long green balloon.

She twisted it into the shape of a rabbit.

She gave it to Jane.

The clown made balloon dogs,

swans, and cats.

She gave me an orange cat.

"Now, I will do my best trick," she said.

"I will make birthday cake disappear."

Not-Me Amy's dad gave the clown

a large piece of cake.

The clown ate the cake.

"I did it," she said. "The cake is gone."

"Yay!" we shouted.

The clown bowed and left the room.

The party was over.

# 3. Bears, Lions, and Giraffes

Parents came to take their children home.

Not-Me Amy's mom and dad

helped the children get their coats.

Jane and I waited in the den for our parents.

Not-Me Amy waited with us.

Then the clown came into the den.

"Where are my clothes?" she asked.

"I came here in regular clothes.

Now they're gone.

They have disappeared."

"Yay!" Jane and Amy shouted.

"No," the clown said. "It's not a trick."

"Before the party

I changed into my clown clothes,"

she said. "I left my regular clothes

in one of the bedrooms.

Now my regular clothes are gone."

"I'll find your clothes," I said.

"I'm a detective."

I took my detective bag and my balloon cat.

"I'll help," Not-Me Amy said.

"I have a detective glass.

It's good for finding things."

We followed the clown out of the den.

"Wait for me," Jane said.

We went to the spare room.

The clown pointed to a chair.

"That's where I left my clothes," she said.

There were no clothes on the chair.

Not-Me Amy looked through her glass.

"Wow," she said. "That's a big chair."

She looked at the clown.

"That's a big red nose," she said.

"Maybe you are just mixed up,"
I said. "Maybe you left your clothes
in another bedroom."

"Maybe you left your clothes
in my room," Not-Me Amy said.

We followed Not-Me Amy to her room.
She had lots of stuffed animals.
Toy bears, lions, and giraffes
were everywhere.

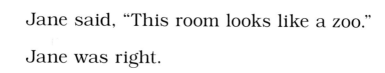

Jane said, "This room looks like a zoo."

Jane was right.

We found lots of animals in the room.

But we didn't find the clown's clothes.

# 4. Maybe I'm Not a Great Detective

"Maybe you're really mixed up,"

Not-Me Amy said.

"Maybe you didn't change your clothes

in my house. Maybe you changed

before you came here."

"No," the clown said.

She shook her head.

The bells on her hat tinkled.

"I changed my clothes in this house."

The clown sat on Not-Me Amy's bed.

"My car keys, wallet, and cell phone
are in the pocket of my pants."
The clown looked
at Not-Me Amy, Jane, and me.
"Isn't one of you
a detective?" she asked.
"Not me," Not-Me Amy said.
"I'm a detective," I said.
"But I need clues to solve a mystery."

I opened my detective bag.

I turned the bag upside down.

My detective things fell onto the bed.

"You'll have to clean that up,"

Not-Me Amy said.

"This is a neat house."

"I'll clean later," I said.

"Right now I need something

to help me solve this mystery."

I looked at my detective glass,
code breaker, and walkie-talkies.

"Hey," I said. "My walkie-talkies told me
how to find the missing clothes."

"Hello," I said into one walkie-talkie.

"Hello" came out the other one.

I told the clown, "We'll call your phone.
When we hear it ringing,
we'll know where to find
your cell phone and your clothes."

Hello

"No, you won't," the clown said.

"The phone is turned off."

I sat on the bed. I had no clues,

and the clown had no regular clothes.

"Jeffrey!" Not-Me Amy's dad called.

"Your father is here."

"I have to go," I told the clown.

"Maybe Amy's mom and dad

can find your things."

I put my detective things in my bag.

I walked to the front door.

I didn't solve this mystery, I thought.

Maybe I'm not a great detective.

# 5. Yes, I Am!

"Look, Dad," I said.

"The clown gave me a balloon cat."

"That's nice," Dad said.

"Where did you put your parka?"

I told Dad that I put it on a chair.

Amy's mom opened the closet.

"I hung it here," she said.

I looked at the chair.

I looked at my parka.

It was hanging in the closet.

"That's it!" I said.

"I just solved another mystery."

I went to Not-Me Amy's room.

I told the clown,

"I know where to find your clothes."

The clown, Not-Me Amy, and Jane

followed me to the spare bedroom.

I opened the closet door and looked in.

I found the clown's clothes.

The clown smiled. "Thank you," she said.

"Now, please excuse me.

I want to get dressed."

We left the spare room.

Not-Me Amy asked, "How did you know

where to find her clothes?"

"I put my parka on a chair," I said.

"Your mom hung it in the closet.

The clown left her clothes on a chair.

I thought that maybe your mom

hung the clown's clothes in a closet, too."

Not-Me-Amy smiled and said,

"Mom and Dad like to keep this house neat."

"Thank you for solving this mystery,"
she said.

"Thank you," I said,

"for inviting me to your party.
I like parties, and I like
solving mysteries."

I smiled. I am a great detective.

Yes, I am!